# ALSO BY ANTHONY DELAUNEY

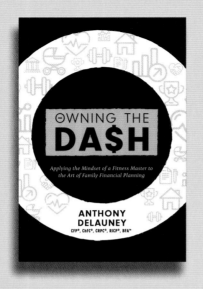

*Owning the Dash: Applying the Mindset of a Fitness Master to the Art of Family Financial Planning*

*Owning the Dash: The No-Regrets Retirement Roadmap*

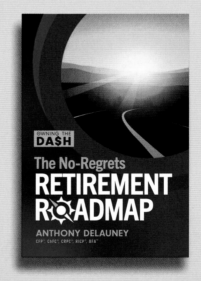

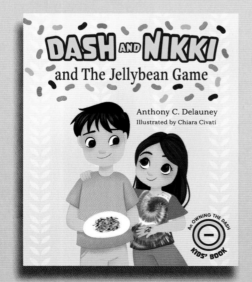

*Dash and Nikki and The Jellybean Game*
(Book 1 in the Owning the Dash Kids' Book series)

To all the moms and dads who know the sadness of goodbye hugs and the joys of hello kisses.

www.mascotbooks.com

*Lilly and May Learn Why Mom and Dad Work*

For more information, please contact:
Mascot Books
620 Herndon Parkway, Suite 320
Herndon, VA 20170
info@mascotbooks.com

Library of Congress Control Number: 2022902668

CPSIA Code: PRT0422A
ISBN- 13: 978-1-63755-292-6

Printed in the United States

# LILLY AND MAY

## Learn Why Mom and Dad Work

Anthony C. Delauney

Illustrated by Chiara Civati

On a weekday morning like so many before,
Lilly and May stood staring out of their front door.

They watched as their father walked away for the day.
He drove off to work, which was his usual way.

As Lilly closed the door, tears trickled from her eye.
May fell down to the floor. They both started to cry.

May looked up at her mom and stuttered between sobs,
"Why do you and Dad leave us each day for your jobs?"

Their mom knelt next to the girls with tissues in hand.
They sprung into her arms like a snapped rubber band.

"You do not need to be sad," she said with a smile.
"Dad and I will be back home in a little while.

Work is something important that we have to do.
It earns the money we need to take care of you."

She walked with them over to the kitchen table
and pulled out a book with a fancy gold label.

"The time has come," she said, "for you to understand.
Money plays a big part in our family plan."

"Money's boring," May said with a pout on her face.
"Not so," said her mom. "It has a purpose and place.

Let's open the book, and together we will see
all of the ways that money helps our family."

"**W**e use our money to buy the food that we eat, the clothes that we wear, even the shoes on your feet!

Money paid for the car that takes us here and there, and everything in our home, including this chair."

The girls' eyes popped open. Their mouths dropped to the floor.
Lilly grabbed the book. "What else do we use it for?"

"The phones," their mom said, "we use to text and to chat.
Without money, we would not have any of that.

The water that freely flows out of your shower.
Electricity that gives our home its power.

The gas that keeps us warm on chilly winter nights.
Money is how we can afford all these delights!"

"It also pays for the jobs other people do.
Let's turn to the next page, and you'll see that it's true.

The doctor, the dentist, even the dog sitter.
Plus the stylist who painted your nails with glitter.

The actors who we watch on our favorite shows.
Your coaches. Your teachers. The list grows and it grows."

Lilly held up her hand. She had something to add.
"What about the scientists who work with our dad?"

"Or Ms. Belle," May said. "The best babysitter ever!"
Their mom chuckled. "That's right! You girls are so clever."

**"A**nd then there are taxes
that we all need to pay
for the services we use each
and every day.

Think of the people on whom
we often depend.
Those who watch over us, like
your dad's Army friend.

The brave police officers who protect and serve.
The firefighters whose courage we can observe.

Librarians, crossing guards, and school directors.
Judges, janitors, and garbage collectors.

And even construction crews who build and repair
the roads and bridges we use to go everywhere.

They all work very hard on the jobs that they do,
so we pay them with our money to say *thank you!*"

"And let us not forget an important To-Do.
We must save some money for our future days, too.

We save for the day when our red car may break down,
or when we take a big trip and fly out of town."

May pointed to the pictures scattered on the wall.
"Like when we travel to see our cousins each fall?"

"That's correct!" her mom cheered. "How did you get so smart?"
"My sister," May said, putting her hand on her heart.

"We save for future schools where you may discover
how to run a business like me, your mother.

And last, we save for the very exciting day
when Dad and I stop working and get to go play."

"**B**ut what money can't buy is the love we feel for you,
and the joy of seeing all the great things you do!

Your dancing, your singing, your giggles, and your smiles.
Your creative new looks and fantastic hairstyles.

Your passions, your stories, and your beautiful dreams.
The games you love to play with our local sports teams.

The world is full of adventure, excitement, and fun,
and by saving and spending, we help everyone."

**"Y**ou don't need to mope when Dad and I go away.
We promise to be home at the end of each day.

When we leave the house, know that we're helping others.
Families like ours, some with sisters *and* brothers.

And we feel sad, too, when we have to say goodbye.
Sometimes Dad and I also feel the urge to cry.

But then we remember: work helps us live better
and enjoy the fun things we all do together."

"So let's have a big hug because now you can see
the many ways that money helps our family.

And when you think us leaving for work isn't fair,
remember that your dad and I work because we care."

May stood up and gave her mom a kiss on the cheek.
"Thank you," she said, "for going to work every week."

Lilly twirled her hair and then tugged her mom's shoulder.
"Can I get a money book, too, when I'm older?"

"You both can," their mom said, reaching for the doorknob.
"But Ms. Belle's here now, so I must leave for my job."

Lilly and May waved as their mom rushed out the door,
the sisters feeling prouder than ever before.

They now know why their mom and dad work hard each day:
to earn the money they use to live and to play.

See if you can match the image to the right category!

## THINGS, JOBS, TAXES, SAVINGS

Furniture
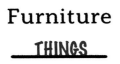 THINGS

 Crossing Guard
_____

 Teacher
_____

Scientist
_____

 Police Officer
_____

 College
_____

Stylist

_____

Garbage Collector

_____

Soldier

_____

 Broken Car

_____

Coach

_____

 Doctor

_____

 Phones

_____

 Librarian

_____

Firefighter _____

 Electricity _____

 Travel _____

Dentist _____

 Babysitter _____

 Food _____

Clothes _____

Judge _____

 Retirement
_____

 Actor
_____

 Dog Sitter
_____

 Gas
_____

 Construction Worker
_____

Water _____

 Principal
_____

 Janitor
_____

# ABOUT THE AUTHOR

Anthony Delauney is a financial advisor based in Raleigh, North Carolina, who has a passion for helping families. He is the founder of Owning the Dash, LLC, an organization dedicated to helping educate and inspire families as they work to achieve their financial goals. His other books include *Owning the Dash: Applying the Mindset of a Fitness Master to the Art of Family Financial Planning, Owning the Dash: The No-Regrets Retirement Roadmap,* and *Dash and Nikki and The Jellybean Game.*

*Lilly and May Learn Why Mom and Dad Work* is Anthony's second book in the Owning the Dash Kids' Book series. With the help of his wife Laura, daughter Abbie, and son Jason, he wrote the book to entertain children of all ages and to teach them an important financial lesson that will help guide them in the years to come. Many more exciting adventures await Lilly, May, and their friends! Anthony, Laura, Abbie, and Jason hope you enjoy the book!

Special thanks to the Jones family! You have always inspired me with your compassion and love for all those around you.